the CRitteR club

Liz and the Sand Castle Contest

by Callie Barkley ♥ illustrated by Marsha Riti

LITTLE SIMON

New York   London   Toronto   Sydney   New Delhi

LITTLE SIMON

An imprint of Simon & Schuster Children's Publishing Division • 1230 Avenue of the Americas, New York, New York 10020 • First Little Simon hardcover edition June 2015 Copyright © 2015 by Simon & Schuster, Inc. All rights reserved, including the right of reproduction in whole or in part in any form. LITTLE SIMON is a registered trademark of Simon & Schuster, Inc., and associated colophon is a trademark of Simon & Schuster, Inc. For information about special discounts for bulk purchases, please contact Simon & Schuster Special Sales at 1-866-506-1949 or business@simonandschuster.com. The Simon & Schuster Speakers Bureau can bring authors to your live event. For more information or to book an event contact the Simon & Schuster Speakers Bureau at 1-866-248-3049 or visit our website at www.simonspeakers.com.
Designed by Laura Roode. The text of this book was set in ITC Stone Informal Std.
Manufactured in the United States of America 0515 FFG   10 9 8 7 6 5 4 3 2 1
Library of Congress Cataloging-in-Publication Data
Barkley, Callie. Liz and the sand castle contest / Callie Barkley ; illustrated by Marsha Riti. — First Little Simon paperback edition. pages cm. — (The Critter Club ; #11)
Summary: As her friends in the Critter Club animal shelter care for colorful aquarium fish, second-grader Liz and her family spend a long weekend at the beach, where Liz rescues a baby octopus and competes with an unfriendly young neighbor in a sand castle contest. [1. Beaches—Fiction. 2. Wildlife rescue—Fiction. 3. Contests—Fiction. 4. Friendship—Fiction.] I. Riti, Marsha, illustrator. II. Title. PZ7.B250585Lg 2015 [Fic]—dc23 2014043217
ISBN 978-1-4814-2406-6 (hc)
ISBN 978-1-4814-2405-9 (pbk)
ISBN 978-1-4814-2407-3 (eBook)

Contents

Chapter 1

To the Beach!

Liz Jenkins peered through the glass side of the fish tank. "I really wish I were a fish right now!" she said.

She and her friends, Ellie, Amy, and Marion, were at The Critter Club. They were standing around an aquarium filled with colorful fish. The girls were pet sitting the fish for a couple of weeks.

"It *would* feel great to go for a swim," Ellie agreed. "Do you think fish *ever* get hot?"

Santa Vista was in the middle of a summer heat wave. Liz would bet it was about ninety-five degrees in Ms. Sullivan's barn. The barn was the headquarters of The Critter Club, the animal rescue shelter the girls had started.

"I forgot how hot it can get here," Marion said. She had just returned from horseback riding camp. "Up in the mountains at camp, it was so cool!"

Amy sighed. "I'm just glad my writing program is inside," she said. "The classroom at the rec center is super air-conditioned!"

Amy sprinkled fish food into the water. The fish raced up to the surface to snatch the crumbs.

"You're lucky," Ellie said to Amy. "Nana Gloria doesn't like turning on the air conditioner." Nana Gloria was Ellie's grandmother. She lived with Ellie's family. "I'm going to melt by the time my parents get back from their trip!" She turned to Liz. "You have to take me with you to Luna Beach tomorrow!"

Liz giggled. "I wish I could take

all three of you!" she replied. "But our car is going to be packed!"

Liz's family was leaving the next day. They had rented a beach cottage for a long weekend. Liz could not wait. Even when it was hot at the beach, there were sea breezes and cool waves. Liz was a strong swimmer. She could body surf all weekend to stay cool.

Liz looked down at the fish. "I'm just sorry I won't be able to help with these guys," Liz said.

"That's okay," Ellie said. "We three can handle them. But we'll miss you, Liz!"

Amy and Marion nodded.

Liz smiled. "Thanks, you guys. And hey, I'll probably meet lots of other fish in the sea!"

Chapter 2

The Boy on the Bike

"Mom?" Liz called from the back-seat. "How much longer until we get there?"

"Just a few more miles!" Liz's mom replied.

Liz loved her family's lake house on Marigold Lake, but she was excited to get to the beach. She'd never been to this one before.

Just as Liz had predicted, the car *was* packed. All the way in the back, there were backpacks and boogie boards. There were bags with Frisbees and paddleball

equipment. There were piles of beach towels. And there were two coolers filled with veggie burgers and tofu dogs. They were the family's favorite cookout foods.

Even the roof rack was full. Liz's older brother, Stewart, was bringing his surfboard. He'd learned to surf the summer before. Already, he was really good at it.

Liz had put her most important things in the little compartment next to her seat: a pad of paper and her case of drawing pencils. Liz loved to draw

and paint. She never went any-
where without her sketchbook.

"I can't wait to get back on my
board!" Stewart said. "I hope the
waves are big at Luna Beach!"

"Well," said Liz, "I can't wait to
swim and boogie board. And build

sand castles! I'm definitely going to build a sand castle."

Liz thought of sand castle-building as an art. She usually made a sketch before she got started. Some days at the beach, she spent hours working on the same sand castle. At home, she had photos of her best ones, taken before the waves had washed them away.

Finally the Jenkins family rolled into town. Liz looked out the window. They passed a playground that looked pretty cool. Liz noticed some kids her age riding bikes. She smiled. She had a feeling this was going to be a fun weekend!

Mrs. Jenkins pulled into the driveway of the cottage. Liz and Stewart raced inside to figure out who got which room. Then they all unloaded the car.

"How about we get into our bathing suits?" Mrs. Jenkins said. "We can spend the rest of the afternoon at the beach."

"I'll pack some sandwiches," Mr. Jenkins added.

The beach was a short walk from the cottage. Mr. and Mrs.

Jenkins carried the beach chairs and umbrella. Stewart lugged the cooler. Liz hurried on ahead with the blanket and a bag of beach toys.

Just before they reached the
beach path, Liz heard a boy's
laugh and the creak of a bike
chain behind her. She turned. A
red-headed boy on a bike whizzed
past her, way too close.

"Whoa!" Liz cried,
jumping back.

The boy
pedaled on.
Liz watched
him as he rode
away. Just for a
second, he turned
his head to look

back at her. Liz thought she saw the
tiniest smile on his face. Almost . . .
a smirk?

Chapter 3

Heads or Tails?

Luna Beach had the clearest water and softest sand of any beach Liz had ever been to.

Right away, she and her family went for a swim. It was almost low tide. The waves were too small for surfing, but just right for *body* surfing. Stewart gave Liz pointers on how to ride a wave all the way in.

Later, Liz's dad read a book. Stewart took a nap under the beach umbrella. Liz and her mom tossed the Frisbee around.

When they got hungry, they sat together on the beach blanket and ate their sandwiches. They watched the sky turn a pink-orange as the sun set. Liz pulled out her sketch-book and colored pencils and made a quick sketch.

Then they started to pack up their stuff. "Not a bad first day at the beach, right?" said Mr. Jenkins.

"And we still have *two more*

before it's time to go home!" Liz added.

On the way back up the beach path, Liz spotted a paper tacked to a fence post. It was flapping in the breeze like a flag. Liz smoothed it out so she could read it.

Sand Castle Contest
this weekend!

Build on Saturday!

Finishing touches and judging on Sunday!

Sign up at the
Luna Beach
lifeguard station
Friday evening ONLY!

Only a few spots left!

Liz gasped. A sand castle contest?! That was perfect for her!

Stewart came over. He read the flyer over Liz's shoulder. "BOR-ing," he said. "Who'd want to build sand castles when they could be surfing? Right, Liz?"

He laughed and elbowed Liz. But then he noticed the dreamy look on Liz's face.

"Oh!" Stewart said. "But *you'd* probably like it."

Liz smiled. She and Stewart were

different in a lot of ways. But he *was* a pretty good brother.

"The last chance to sign up is tonight," Liz pointed out. "I'm probably too late."

Stewart reread the flyer. "The lifeguard station is right down there," he said, pointing down the beach. "Come on, I'll go with you to check it out!"

Liz and Stewart told their parents their plan.

Then they hurried down the beach while their mom and dad walked back to the cottage.

When they reached the lifeguard station, Liz saw a woman sitting at a table out front. She had a clipboard. Stewart hung back while Liz went over to the table.

"Hi!" Liz said. "Is this where I sign up for—"

"Excuse me!" a voice shouted, interrupting. A

boy ran up to talk to the woman—
as if Liz wasn't even there. "I want
to sign up for the contest."

Liz turned. It was that red-headed
boy—the one on the bike.

The woman looked down at her clipboard. "Oh dear," she said. "I'm afraid we have only one spot left." She smiled at Liz, then at the boy.

Well, this is awkward, thought Liz. She tried to lighten things up with a joke. "Flip a coin for it?" she suggested. Liz figured the boy would say she should take the spot. After all, she *did* get there first.

But the boy stared back at her without smiling. "Okay," he said. "I call tails!"

Chapter 4

Critter Creativity

Liz was speechless. She'd only been kidding. But this kid was serious! Liz looked over at her brother, thinking maybe he had advice. But Stewart was poking at something in the sand. He hadn't heard what was going on.

At that moment, the lady's cell phone rang. She answered it. "Uh huh. Mm-hmm. Okay, no problem," she was saying. "Thanks for call- ing." When she hung up, she crossed something off her clipboard.

"Good news!" she announced with a smile. "Someone who signed up can't make it. So I have two spots after all!"  She slid her clipboard and pen across the table so they could add their names.

The boy snatched up the pen.

Liz watched as he wrote his name down: *Tommy Cook.*

Then he hurried off without another word.

Huh, Liz thought as she added her name to the signup sheet. *Not the friendliest boy in the world.*

Still, Liz tried to think the best of people. Maybe he was just shy. Not everybody made friends easily.

Back at the cottage, Liz used the phone to call Ellie in Santa Vista. She was wondering how the fish were doing. Ellie reported that the fish had a new best friend: Ms. Sullivan's dog, Rufus!

"It's the funniest thing," Ellie said. "Rufus sat in front of the fish tank most of the afternoon today. He was just watching them swim back and forth!"

Liz laughed. "Rufus?" she said. "Sitting still?"

"I know!" Ellie replied. "He's

usually a fur ball of energy. But watching the fish seems to make him really . . . *calm*." Ellie giggled. "I thought he was going to fall asleep."

Then Liz told Ellie about the sand castle contest. Ellie wished her good luck. "I wish we could be there to see your masterpiece!" Ellie exclaimed.

When Liz got off the phone, she sighed. She did miss her friends and

The Critter Club. But she was really excited about the contest.

She got out her sketchbook and a pencil. Her pencil hovered above the paper. What would she make her sand castle look like? Then an idea came to her.

Ms. Sullivan's barn: The Critter Club!

Chapter 5

The Contest

The next morning, Liz's family got to Luna Beach bright and early. They spread out their blanket and put up their umbrella. Liz took all the buckets, shovels, and sand tools they had. Then her mom pointed out the contest area down the beach.

"We'll come down in a little

while to check on you," her mom said.

"And cheer you on," her dad added.

"Good luck, Liz!" Stewart shouted as he ran into the water with his surfboard.

As she headed off, Liz felt a little nervous, but mostly excited! It was fun to go check in by herself. Even though she could wave to her parents down the beach, this felt like *her* adventure.

In the contest area, squares of sand were marked off with red string that was staked in the ground. Lots of people were already there. There

were other kids Liz's age, plus older kids and grown-ups of all ages.

Liz found the lady from the signup table. She remembered Liz right away. "My name is Melinda," she said to Liz. "Follow me!"

She led Liz to a plot of sand at the end of a row. "This will be your area for building," Melinda said. "Use the sand

within your square. Plus, everyone can take sand from over there." Melinda showed Liz a big sand pile in the middle of the contest area.

Melinda checked her watch. "We'll be starting in five minutes. Good luck!"

Liz thanked her. She dumped out her sand tools and then looked around. For the first time, she noticed who was in the square right next to her: Tommy Cook.

He was setting
up his things.
Tommy looked over
in Liz's direction. Liz gave
a small wave. Tommy looked
away without waving back.
Liz shrugged. She reached into

the pocket of her beach cover-up.
She pulled out her sand castle
sketch. Then Liz found a few small
rocks on the beach. She laid the
sketch on the sand and used the
rocks to keep it from blowing away.

She looked over at Tommy again.

He didn't seem to have a sketch or a blueprint. Liz took a step toward him. "You're Tommy, right?" she called. "I'm Liz."

Liz wasn't sure if he'd heard her. He didn't look up.

Liz called out a little louder. "What kind of castle are you going to build?"

As she spoke, Tommy picked up a bucket and ran off. He went down to the water to fill it up.

Liz was sure he heard her that time.

Just as Tommy was coming back, Melinda blew a whistle. "Ready, set, build!" she called out.

At the same moment, a gust of wind came down the beach. It blew Liz's sketch out from under the rocks.

"Oh no!" Liz cried as it rolled down the beach like a tumbleweed. She chased after it.

As she did, she was pretty sure she heard Tommy laughing.

Chapter 6

It's a . . . Baby Octopus!

Liz caught her sketch, weighted it down with heavier rocks, and got started on her sand castle. For the next hour—at least—she forgot Tommy was even there. Liz was an artist, focused on her work.

She piled up sand to make the main structure.

She used her small shovel to form

the edges of the barn.

She added details using a stick.

When Liz was happy with the barn, she started making sand animals around it. She began with a dog—Rufus, of course!

Then Liz made some of the other animals they had taken care of at The Critter Club.

She made a bunny, a kitten, a turtle, and a pig.

Liz stood back and examined her work. She had more to do. But she was pretty happy with it so far!

She looked over at Tommy's castle and did a double take. The walls of his castle looked like real stone!

"Wow!" she said to him. "That looks awesome!"

This time, Tommy did look up. "Thanks," he mumbled. Then he frowned and went right back to work.

Liz looked at what he was working on. It was a sand horse. But as he was forming the head, the whole horse collapsed. Tommy's shoulders fell. He sighed impatiently.

"I'm making animals for my sand castle too," she said. "Do you want some help with that?"

Tommy looked over at Liz's sculpture. "You call that a castle?" he said. "It looks like a plain old barn to me."

Liz had to try extra hard not to feel insulted. *Okay, that came out sounding really rude,* she thought. *But he just doesn't get it.*

"It's not just a barn," Liz said. "It's The Critter Club. My friends and I started it. It's an animal rescue shelter in my town."

Once again, Liz wasn't sure Tommy was listening. He was trying to build the sand horse back up. It fell apart again.

"Can I help?" Liz asked again. "If you—"

"I don't want

your help!" Tommy burst out. Frustrated, he picked up a bucket and tossed it away. The sea breeze caught it. It veered off in the direction of Liz's sculpture.

Thump! The bucket landed on top of sand Rufus, flattening him. Liz gasped.

Tommy looked at her sheepishly. "Whoops," he said. "Sorry."

Liz *almost* said, "That's okay." But she didn't. Instead, she walked away, down to the ocean. She needed a break.

Liz dipped her feet in the water and took some deep breaths. She knew Tommy hadn't meant to hit her sculpture. But she was annoyed!

Especially since Tommy didn't even offer to help her fix Rufus!

Just then, something in the shallow water caught Liz's eye. At first, it looked like a small piece of seaweed.

Liz looked closer. Whatever it was had tiny circular markings. They looked like . . . suction cups!

"A baby octopus!" Liz said out loud.

Chapter 7

Liz to the Rescue!

Liz's heart pounded in her chest. She loved unusual animals. And an octopus was definitely unusual! Of course, she'd seen them in aquariums. But Liz had never seen an octopus in the ocean—in the wild!

Then Liz realized why. Didn't octopuses like deep water?

She noticed the octopus didn't

seem to be swimming. It was being carried in and out with the tiny waves.

Oh no! thought Liz. Worry crept in, taking the place of her excitement. *Is this octopus in trouble?*

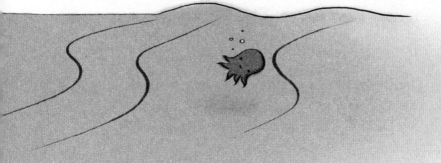

Liz raced up to her sand sculpture. She grabbed the biggest bucket
she had. Then she sprinted back
to the water. She had to help that
octopus!

Very gently, Liz scooped the

octopus up into the bucket, along with a lot of water. She carried it a few steps farther into the ocean. Then Liz lowered the octopus back into the water. She watched to see if it would start to swim.

"Come on, little octopus," she whispered. "You can do it."

But it drifted, motionless.

"What are you doing?" a voice called from the beach. It was Tommy. He was standing at the water's edge.

Liz lifted up the octopus in the bucket again. She carried the bucket out of the ocean. She didn't say

anything to Tommy as she started walking down the beach toward her family's blanket.

Tommy walked alongside her. He peered into the bucket. "What is that? What are you doing with it?"

Liz explained it was an octopus, and it seemed to be sick. "I'm going to call my friend's mom. She's a veterinarian. Maybe she'll know how to help it."

Tommy stopped. He watched Liz walk on with the heavy bucket. "But what about your sculpture?" he called after her. "Aren't you going to finish?"

Liz shrugged. Maybe she'd have time to finish Sunday morning. All of a sudden, she didn't care so much about the contest.

Liz's dad dialed the number for Dr. Purvis's vet clinic on his cell phone. He handed the phone to Liz so she could explain the situation.

"Hmm, this a tricky one," Dr. Purvis told Liz. "If the octopus is sick, there's not much you can do. But maybe it's just weak for some reason. In the water, it could get into trouble. It might help to keep it out of the ocean—just until it gets its strength back."

Dr. Purvis advised Liz to keep the octopus in seawater in the biggest container they had. "I would put it back in the ocean tomorrow.

Hopefully, it will be stronger by then," she said.

Back at the cottage, Liz's mom found a kiddie pool in a storage shed. With Stewart's help, Liz brought buckets of ocean water up from the beach. They used them to fill the pool. Then they lowered the octopus into it. The octopus drifted out into the pool.

Liz set up a beach chair next to the pool. She sat down to keep the octopus company.

She had followed all
of Dr. Purvis's instruc-
tions. Now all she could
do was wait . . . and
hope.

Chapter 8

Windy Worries

After dinner, Liz's family went out to play mini-golf. She'd wanted to stay with the octopus. "Come on, Liz," her dad had said. "We'll only be gone an hour or so."

Now, on the eighth hole, Liz checked her watch. They'd been gone forty-five minutes! She really wanted to get back.

But it was Liz's turn to putt. Distracted, she swung way too hard. Her ball launched off the green. A sudden gust of wind lifted it farther. It sailed off in the direction of the first hole.

The ball bounced off a rock. Then it hit a boy on the back of his leg. "OW!" he cried out.

Liz hurried over. "I'm sooo sorry!" she exclaimed. "I—"

The boy turned. It was Tommy! He and his parents were just starting their game.

"That kind of hurt!" Tommy said sternly.

"I really didn't mean to," Liz said. "Really, *really*." She looked at Tommy's parents. Liz tried a smile, but she was embarrassed.

"Not to worry," Tommy's mom said kindly. "No harm done."

Before Liz could say anything else, another wind gust blew the baseball cap off her head. She hurried after it. She grabbed it right before it landed in a water trap.

When she turned, Tommy and his family were moving on to the second hole.

Liz returned to her family on the last hole. They'd been busy taking their turns. They hadn't seen Liz's run-in with Tommy.

The next morning, Liz watched her step as she walked down to

the beach. She was carrying the octopus in a bucket of seawater. It looked stronger today!

Liz's family got their beach spot set up again. Then Liz passed the bucket off to her parents. They were going to babysit the octopus for the

morning. Meanwhile, Liz would go down the beach to finish her sculpture. After the contest, if the octopus seemed ready, they'd release it together.

Liz got to the contest area a few minutes late. She hurried along the row of sand plots to her own at the very end. She passed some amazing sculptures! One girl was working on a lighthouse. An older man was adding balconies to a skyscraper. There was even an *igloo* made of sand!

Tommy was already in his square, hard

at work. Liz looked away when he glanced up. She still felt pretty embarrassed about the mini-golf.

Then Liz stopped in her tracks. She was staring at her sand plot.

The red strings were still there, marking her square. But her sculpture was not! The barn, the animals, everything—gone. Instead, there were just lumps and drifts of sand where all her hard work had been.

What happened? thought Liz. *Who would do this?*

Chapter 9

Tommy's Idea

Liz looked over at Tommy. He was watching her with a strange look on his face. To Liz, it seemed like he was waiting to see what she would do next.

Liz couldn't believe it. *Did he wreck my sculpture? On purpose?* she wondered.

Liz tried to stay calm. But Tommy

had been so mean to her the day before. And now *this*?

She marched over to Tommy's square. "Did *you* do this?" she demanded. She didn't wait for an answer. "Hitting you with the golf ball was an *accident*. You did this on *purpose*!"

"Wait! Hold on a second!" Tommy cried.

Liz felt a hand on her shoulder. She whirled around.

Melinda was there. She looked apologetic.

"I'm so sorry about your castle, Liz," she said, shaking her head. "I noticed it this morning. One of the beach lifeguards did too. He said the winds were really strong over here last night." Melinda pointed out a rocky seawall between the beach and some sand dunes. "Yours is the only sand plot that wasn't shielded by that wall."

Liz looked sheepishly at Tommy. She felt bad for yelling at him.

Melinda went on. "I wish we could have you rebuild everything," she said. "But I'm afraid we don't have time. I'm so sorry, Liz."

Liz's heart fell. She was so proud of her barn. She'd really worked hard on it! Now it wouldn't even be seen by the judges.

"I understand," Liz said sadly. "I guess I'll gather up my tools."

Liz noticed Tommy watching and listening. He opened his mouth to say something. Then he closed it again. Liz was sure whatever he had to say wasn't very nice. *I really hope he keeps it to himself,* she thought.

But suddenly Tommy blurted it out.

"She can help me finish mine," he said.

Liz froze. She definitely hadn't heard that right.

Melinda smiled. "What good sportsmanship! That's so nice of you!" She turned to Liz. "Would you like to do that?"

Liz didn't know what to say. Was Tommy just teasing? He *looked* like he meant it. But . . .

"Are you sure?" Liz asked Tommy.

Tommy nodded. "Yeah," he said. "I think I could use some more

sand animals around the castle."
He smiled. Not a smirk this time,
but a real, warm smile.

Liz smiled back. She *did* really
want to take part in the contest.

"Okay!" she cried. She grabbed
her sand tools and hopped into
Tommy's square.

It Takes Two

Melinda blew her whistle. "Time's up!" she called out.

Liz and Tommy put their sand tools down. They stepped away from their castle.

Liz saw her family watching on the sidelines. She ran over and told them what had happened to her sand sculpture. Then she called

Tommy over so she could introduce them. "Tommy let me help him with *his* castle," Liz said.

"Oh, sweetheart," Mrs. Jenkins said to Liz. "That's too bad about your sculpture."

"Yeah," said Stewart. "But that castle you guys made is awesome! It has a ton of details!"

Liz looked over at their castle. They had added lots of horses guarding the outside. Liz had shown Tommy a trick—carving them from a block of wet sand instead of building them up from nothing.

105

They even had time to add a mini version of The Critter Club barn as a stable for the horses!

Liz watched as three judges walked around it. They were writing something on their clipboards. Liz wished she knew *what*!

"Hey, Tommy," Liz said as they stood waiting to hear who won.

"How come you didn't want my help yesterday?"

Tommy looked down and lightly kicked some sand. "I'm sorry. I...I was really nervous," Tommy explained. "Every summer I enter this contest. And I've never won. Not even close!

I just really wanted to win, finally—all on my own."

Liz nodded. "Well, it was really nice of you to let me work on your castle."

"I never could have made those horses by myself," Tommy replied.

Finally, the judges were ready. Everybody gathered around to hear Melinda announce their decisions. "The judges have awarded ribbons for first, second, and third place," said Melinda.

The third-place winner was the older man who had built the skyscraper.

"He's really good," Tommy told Liz as they clapped. "He's been building sand castles for years."

Second place went to a young woman. Melinda mentioned that she was a well-known artist in Luna Beach.

"And in first place," Melinda said, "congratulations to . . ."

Liz held her breath.

"Tess Munroe!" Melinda called out. A woman came running up to claim her blue ribbon. She was jumping and clapping! Liz couldn't help feeling happy for her.

Liz shrugged and smiled at Tommy. "Oh well," Liz said.

"Yeah," Tommy said glumly. "That first-place castle *is* good. It has a drawbridge and everything!"

As they turned to go, Melinda's voice rang out again.

"And one more prize!" she said. "The judges awarded an honorable mention . . . to Liz Jenkins and Tommy Cook!"

Liz looked at Tommy. Tommy looked at Liz. Then they both started jumping up and down like crazy.

"Whoo-hoo!" Liz cried.

"Yes!" shouted Tommy. "This is the closest I've ever come to winning!"

Melinda came over. She had a green ribbon for each of them. "Congratulations!" she said. "And great teamwork, you two!"

Liz's dad took a photo of Liz and Tommy in front of their castle.

Then Tommy came down to the water with

Liz and her family. They had the bucket with the octopus, and it was time to let it go!

"I hope it'll be all right," Liz said as she lowered the bucket into the ocean.

Right away, the octopus propelled itself out of the bucket and into the sea. Within seconds, it had disappeared into deeper water.

"You're welcome!" Liz shouted after it with a laugh.

"Looks like it'll be just fine," Mr. Jenkins said.

"It's really lucky you found it," Tommy said to Liz. "And that you know so much about animals. Sand animals *and* real animals!"

Tommy's parents were calling him from down the beach. "Gotta go," he said. "Maybe I'll see you around!"

Liz shook her head. "We're going home tomorrow," she said. "But maybe I'll see you here next summer?"

Tommy nodded. "We could have a sand castle rematch!" he said.

"You're on!" Liz replied.

Read on for a sneak peek at
the next Critter Club book:

#12

Marion Takes Charge

"Here, Gabby," Marion Ballard said to her little sister. "I'll do that for you."

"No, I can do it!" Gabby replied. She was at the front door, tying her shoes. Marion thought she was doing it way too slowly.

Mrs. Ballard was waiting in the car. Marion checked her watch. It was 8:35. School started at 8:45, and the drive was eight minutes long. If they didn't get going, they'd be late!

Finally, Gabby was ready. They rushed outside.

Phew! thought Marion as her mom backed out of the driveway.

Marion made sure she had everything. She had her lunch box. She had her sneakers for gym. She peeked inside her homework folder. Yep, she had her homework.

"Got your lunch, Gabby?" Marion asked her sister.

Gabby nodded. "Your home-work?" Marion said.

Gabby nodded again. She was in kindergarten. She usually had a short math work sheet and some reading homework.

"Your reading folder?" Marion asked.

Gabby's eyes went wide in alarm. "I forgot to read the new book in my reading folder!"